D0690131

For Liz, who loves owls ~ C. P.

To my uncle Edvard Kristensen ~ T. M.

This edition published by Scholastic Inc., 557 Broadway; New York, NY 10012,
by arrangement with Little Tiger Press.
SCHOLASTIC and associated logos are trademarks and/or registered trademarks of Scholastic Inc.
Scholastic Canada Ltd.; Markham, Ontario

First published in the United States by Good Books, Intercourse, PA 17534, 2008
Original edition published in English by Little Tiger Press,
an imprint of Magi Publications, London, England, 2008

Text copyright © Caroline Pitcher 2008
Illustrations copyright © Tina Macnaughton 2008

All rights reserved. No part of this book may be reproduced in any manner,
except for brief quotations in critical articles or reviews, without permission.

ISBN-13: 978-1-84506-732-8
ISBN-10: 1-84506-732-0

Printed in China

2 4 6 8 10 9 7 5 3 1

The Littlest Owl

Caroline Pitcher   Tina Macnaughton

Deep inside a willow tree
were four white eggs.

One egg hatched,
then two, then three,
deep inside a willow tree.

Three owlets blinked at the last white egg.
One said, "It's very quiet in there."
Two said, "Maybe the baby can't get out."
Three said, "Maybe the egg is empty.
Maybe there isn't a baby inside."

"There is! Whoo-whooo, there's me,
there's me!" cried the last owlet,
struggling free.
	And there sat Four, so short
and small, a downy, white ball.

Deep inside the willow tree, feeding time was such
a scramble. One, Two, and Three snatched the food.
They gobbled and gulped and blinked at Four.

One said, "Oh dear. He's short."

Two said, "Oh dear. He's so small."

Three said, "He'll never grow big and strong
like us."

"I will!" cried Four. "Just wait and see."

He scratched around in
the bottom of the nest
and found a worm.

One, Two, and Three grew more each day.
They jostled and trampled Four, so short
and small, the downy, white ball.

Mother Owl hooted, "Don't squash
him, please!"

"I'm fine, Ma," he chirped. "I don't mind
being small at all."

One, Two, and Three were changing
fast. They shuffled out onto a branch.
They stretched their wings and
launched themselves into the air.
There they fluttered to and fro,
as soft as moths around the tree.
  Four called, "I'll fly too,
whoo-whooo, whoo-whooo."

Four hopped up and down along
the branch. He spread his short
wings wide and cried, "Wait for
me. I'm coming with you!"
But Four couldn't fly, no matter
how hard he tried.

All night long,

    Four bobbed and bounced. All day long, he fluttered

      and flapped. "I will fly," he cried. "I will! I will!"

        But he never even left the branch.

          When dusk fell,

           Four crept back inside

           the tree and tumbled

           into sleep.

Deep inside the willow tree, the owlets snuggled up and slept. But in the woods the wind rose up. It gathered together a terrible storm that whirled around the willow tree. The tree was old. It groaned. It creaked.

"Wake up, wake up!" screeched
   Mother Owl. "The willow tree will crack in two!"
      The sleepy owlets struggled out. One by one they
leapt and flew, and battled with the raging wind.
      "Come quickly, Four!" cried One.
      "What if he blows away?" cried Two.
      "What if he still can't fly?" cried Three.

The wind blew Four's downy feathers flat.
It bounced him like a small white ball and tried
to push him from the tree.

He stretched and strained, and flapped and
cried, "I will do it too, whoo-whooo. Yes, I'm
last and very small. But I'll never give up at all."

He hurled himself high into the air . . .

. . . and he flew
and flew
and flew!